The Black Medallion

Jon M. Jefferson

THE BLACK MEDALLION

The rain slowed, then came to a stop as dawn's light broke through the clouds. The fog was rolling in, shrouding the streets in its embrace. The smoke billowing around the trains added substance to the mists. Mornings in the stations were often a blur, a place of shadows.

As the train pulled into the station the throng of people braced themselves, ready for the mad rush to board. This was only the first boarding of the day. The "earlies" headed to the mines and farms to start their daily cycles. With an ear piercing screech the train announced its arrival in the station. The crowd pushed on board as the night workers pushed off the other side. The normal exchange.

He checked the clock then swung from his perch to move to a new vantage point. In the chilly morning mists, it paid to keep moving. Otherwise muscles could cramp up when you needed them most.

He moved to the market side of the station. The crowds on market day were easy to blend with. He might not always find coin on market day but he could always find food. The smells wafting from the sweets vendors caused his stomach to rebel against further progress.

Fighting through the press of bodies he bumped into a fat man also fighting through the crowd. "Out of my way whelp!" The man pushed Tisdan aside, spinning him out of his way. When he turned back he saw the fat man fall forward with a dagger protruding from the back of his neck.

Tisdan melded back into the crowd. The crowd that now surged around the body of the dead fat man. Though it wasn't a planned distraction it was a sure way to allow him to sneak off, away from prying eyes. How he had managed to throw the dagger true caught him by surprise. This was not part of his training with Jaktor. Most of their current training was in self-preservation. Ways to defend yourself and avoid notice. This had been an assassin's move.

As he was moving further away from the scene he felt a strange weight in his hand. He had forgotten about the purse he removed from the fat man's belt when he bumped into him. The man would no longer be needing it anyway. He slipped the pouch into his belt then moved into the shadows behind a loading dock. From the dock, he returned to his perch.

Again, able to watch over the station he noticed the crowd begin to thin. Another body in low town, forgotten after it fell. A few stragglers were left to strip the body of anything of value. This was their way of "helping." A short time later a crew from the station arrived and lifted the body to a stretcher. They pushed their way through the crowd toward the rail office.

Tisdan pulled the pouch out and emptied the contents into his hand. Not too bad for this time of morning. A couple of silver coins, also a strange medallion, were the better part of what it contained. There were markings on the medallion in an odd script, no resemblance to anything he had seen before.

The metal had a warmth different than the coins he normally sought. It was not something he would be able to spend outright. If he was lucky his fence might be able to give him a few bits for it at any rate. He slipped it into his pouch with the rest of the coins then tossed the empty purse into the distance.

Growing up in low-town, if you wanted to take the trains anywhere else you had to learn how to work the system. Workers had passes to get to and from their stations. These passes were marked with destinations and could only be used for "to and from." To pass within the city special passes were required. Tisdan had a fake pass that allowed him to travel during high traffic times. It worked for quick looks. But later in the morning when the shift transfers have already been done, the inspectors would have more time to look at his pass.

On a good day, he could find an unoccupied cabin he could slip into and hide in until he reached his stop. But other days it paid to be creative. With the right timing, he could talk his way through a bad situation and come out on top.

He boarded the train and found a seat close to the cabins. The conductor was in one of the cars further ahead. They tended to check the cabins last. Passengers who could afford a cabin would not be getting off in low-town or mid-town. The train jerked forward, building speed as it pulled away from the station. He slipped through a thin crowd that had come from the last moments of the market that day.

He crossed from the low-rent car into the cabin car, the hall deserted. Looking back the inspector had made it into the car he just left. There would not be much time before he had to find a home. After a quick listen, he found a quiet cabin. He pushed it open and slipped inside.

He came face to face with a young woman sitting by the cabin window. Though she wore a clean white sun dress, wide brimmed sun hat with a parasol at her side, it was the book she had closed, holding her place with her finger, that caught his attention. She smiled at him, her eyes alight with curiosity. "Can I help you?"

Tisdan, quick to play the part. "Ticket?"

Still smiling, she said, "I have already had it checked." She stood up. Though she appeared younger, she was still a few inches taller than him. "I do believe you may wish to move into the privy if you don't want them to catch you."

Once inside he heard a knock at the main door. There was little sound as it was opened, muffled voices come from the main cabin. The door closed again, and then a knock at the privy door a few moments later.

They spent the ride till mid-town in light conversation. She did not ask who he was or why he snuck into her cabin and revealed nothing of herself. They talked of the weather and state of the train system over tea and cakes as if this had been a daily occurrence. Tisdan felt a bit off but didn't want to call attention to it and didn't want it to end.

When the train pulled into the mid-town station he stepped toward the cabin door and bid her, "adieu."

She stopped him with a hand on his shoulder and pressed a coin into his hand. "I wish you well in your travels." She smiled and sat back down.

Tisdan pocketed the coin without looking at it, smiled, then melded with the passengers disembarking. He turned to watch the train pull away from the station, loaded with new passengers heading to new destinations. In the shadows he pulled the coin from his pocket. The gold shone smartly back at him, worth so much more than he can pilfer in his best weeks.

He absently slipped it into a different pocket of his shirt. The sparkle of the coin had lost its luster when he remembered her smile. Something about it had given him a chill but he couldn't shake it, couldn't get it out of his head.

Little light shone out from the inside of the pub. Shaper stones lined the walls in regular intervals to keep the world inside separate from the outside. As Tisdan looked up and down the street, he saw little more than typical day traffic for midtown. Most spent their time around the shops further down the road. The pub didn't advertise and you wouldn't find anyone loitering around the outside for long. Arnessa's was popular, for reasons beyond its ability to pull in street traffic.

He turned back to the pub entrance, pushed the door open, and slipped through. A large metallic arm barred him from stepping beyond the entryway.

M Ton, the gate keeper, was always on duty and never missed a mark. He held the post well, could not be bribed, and few were willing to try their hand at taking him down. The metal man felt nothing but the dedication to his job. He towered over Tisdan, and stood twice as wide.

Tisdan pulled at the chain around his neck to flash the bauble dangling at its end. He looked at the behemoth expectantly without saying a word.

Copper, lidless eyes flashed with an electric spark at the sight of the bauble. M Ton lowered its arm. "Mind yourself." The voice, a dull echo.

The lighting inside wasn't the best, enough to know what was set in front of you when your food was delivered. In another setting, it could be called mood lighting. In Arnessa's the sparse lighting spread ominous shadows across the tables. Booths along both walls were dark rich woods and leather. Tables were placed intermittently through the center of the room before the bar along the back wall.

Mr. Swintle held his own private booth to the right of the bar; a walled booth which afforded the most privacy available in the entire bar. He had no guards. Weapons were not allowed in Arnessa's, M Ton made sure of it.

Swintle kept odd hours, but he was one of the few fences that Tisdan could count on to know the random odd, like the medallion. He didn't expect much but anything was better than nothing.

Tisdan stepped up to the bar and placed a coin down. Without looking directly at him, one of the faucet jockeys pulled a pint and set it in front of him. He was not even halfway through Arnessa's cheap when he felt the compulsion for the booth.

He crossed the barrier, and stepped into a different world. Crushed red velvet and soft oak stood in stark contrast to the dark leather and deeply stained woods in the pub proper. But that wasn't the part that stood out. He had stepped into a pocket dimension, a place created through the aether. The wooden barrier was the doorway to Swintle's home.

Dressed in a bright silk robe with extensive embroidery, Swintle lounged on large pillows. A girl in little more than a sirik, a chain that hobbled her ankles to her wrists, kneeled beside him pouring red liquid from a decanter into the goblet in his hand.

"I had a feeling I would see you soon." He held out his hand, palm at the ready. "Hand it here."

"Wh..what?" Tisdan had caught the eye of the girl, only briefly. She quickly turned away, a part of the background.

"Let me see it," Swintle had an edge to his voice. "I have little time for foolishness."

He pulled the amulet from his belt, glanced at it then placed it into Swintle's hand. Hefting the weight of the amulet, he turned it casually back and forth. As he flipped it over his eyebrow lifted, his face opened in awe. With his free hand, he traced the lettering on the back side. "Where did you get this?"

"It was in a purse earlier today."

"I can't help you."

"What do you mean?"

Swintle's voice changed slightly just a bit higher and more harried than it had been a moment ago. "Take it and go."

Tisdan hadn't heard the footsteps behind him until it was too late. A strong fist at the back of his shirt lifted him from the floor. As he Struggled to turn he saw the rest of M Ton lift him back into the bar. "Why?" No reply was offered. The entrance had closed in mist. M Ton threw him into the street, then turned back to the pub, and shut the door behind him.

Tisdan picked himself up and stepped briskly out of the way of an approaching carriage. After he dusted himself off he examined the amulet. It looked different than it had earlier. The amulet was the same one but something about it wasn't quite the same as it was before going into the pub. This would take a bit more to figure out than he originally thought.

Tisdan caught the train back to low-town. He had broken the gold with regret, but the thought passed through his mind only briefly. Swintle had never thrown him out before. Though that wasn't the oddest part of the morning.

He had killed the man. No thought, pure instinct, he had killed that man. This return trip on the train had taken the longer path around the city. Lost in thought he hadn't noticed when he boarded. It left him with nothing but time, and his thoughts. Thoughts that kept returning to the knife as it left his hand and the medallion that he carried in his waistcoat pocket.

Or no longer in his pocket but in his hand. He couldn't remember pulling it from his sash. His thumb throbbed with irritation where he had been rubbing the amulet's edge.

The glyphs were clearer, a language he couldn't understand but he could pick out subtle meaning in their placement. He slipped it back into his sash and looked out the window to get his bearings as the train pulled out of another station.

It had been a short stop, with few passengers disembarking. A tall man in a dark suit sat down in the seat opposing his. Tisdan gave him a quick once over. The threading on his suit-coat looked new and clean. His top hat settled in the seat next to him, in his lap was a black cane with a large blue gem embedded in the handle.

"You have been traveling quite a bit today," the man said.

"Excuse me?"

"You have not been easy to find." The man removed his thin leather gloves and placed them in his lap. Gems in the rings on each of his hands held a soft glow.

"I beg your forgiveness sir, but I don't think we've been properly introduced." Tisdan tipped his hat. "How might I help you?"

The man looked him over and reached into his overcoat. He pulled out a silver card case, then loosed a card. As he Handed the card to Tisdan he said, "I represent a party interested in an item you have in your possession."

Tisdan slipped the card into a vest pocket, then stood up. "I think you may have mistaken me for someone else."

As he stepped away the man grabbed his wrist. The touch carried an uncomfortable warmth. "We will not wait long for you."

The door to his apartment stood ajar when he arrived. The deadbolt had been severed, sliced clean through. Tisdan pushed the door open from the side, and did a side look around the frame to see if anyone was still inside.

The apartment was a single room like many in low town, a ten by ten cubicle. Tisdan's apartment had a desk that he used for working on most of his tools. At least it used to. The desk draw was pulled out, its contents scattered around the room. The desk broken, the pieces scattered around the room. The palette he slept on had been flipped and shoved against the wall.

The break-in at his apartment wasn't a major thing in and of itself. He didn't spend much time there so it was almost expected that someone might try to claim the space. But this was more than just an encroachment on territory. Someone was looking for the amulet.

Tisdan pulled the amulet out of his sash and set it on the table in front of Jak. "Ever see anything like this before?"

Using a knife Jak spun it around and then flipped it over. "Where you get it?"

Tisdan watched him for a sign of recognition, a glimmer of an idea. "Station earlier. It was different." He settled back in the chair, breathing out a heavy sigh. "The mark is dead."

Lifting it in the air with the knife, he brought it closer to eye level. "I have heard rumors, but nothing specific. Heard about some mucking about in a station." Setting it down he focused on Tisdan. "You did it?"

"Not sure what happened." He kept his eyes level with Jak's. "There was no thought. I had the purse, pushed past and then turned to see the man fall." Clearing his throat, he glanced out the window. "I didn't stick around."

Jak went into the small kitchen. Cupboard doors squeaked and glasses clinked while he rooted around. He returned with a bottle and a couple shot glasses. "Something is happening." He opened the bottle and filled both glasses. "Something big, and you found your way into it."

"Swintle looked at this and kicked me out." He grabbed the amulet back and slid it into his sash. "Didn't give me a chance to move on my own. M Ton threw me out."

Jak picked up the glass and held it under his nose inhaling deeply. Closing his eyes, he downed the shot and poured another. "I know a guy," he said. "He might be able to help."

He felt out of place. Jak had directed him to a shaper that owed him a favor. A better lead, than any he had on his own, it could be his only chance to decipher the amulet's glyphs. The trouble was finding the guy's shop in hightown.

High town was the Shaper's showplace. Aether lights lit the night streets. The glow from the lights gave off shadows a bit differently than those from gas lamps. The shadows from the gas lamps danced and swayed with the rhythm of the burning gas, they felt alive. This felt sterile, an unlife.

The feeling grew more foreboding by the horseless cabs moving throughout the streets, another shaper addition. Powered by aether the cab traffic flowed steady, hustling passengers throughout their various destinations. The streets were clean, and again felt more bereft of life than elsewhere. Although it was just past dusk, Tisdan found it odd that there were no children playing in the streets or on the sidewalks.

He stepped to the curb and a cab pulled up beside him. The door opened and he stepped inside. There was no driver. "12 Flickman Avenue," he said to the empty air, and the cab was in motion. He watched through the window as the cab drove on. How could this have become so different than the world he grew up in. After a ten-minute trip through the city the cab stopped in front of a two-story building, and the passenger door popped open.

The two-story building had seen better days. Few buildings in high town fell into this sad state of repair. The brickwork around the doorway showed its age. The door itself was solid, just as the walls of the building on the first floor, there were no windows till you came to the second floor. No signage hung on the facade of the building to give a clue of who or what could be found inside.

Tisdan knocked on the door, and looked around the deserted street. He knocked again, still no sounds issued from within. His patience gone, he turned the knob. The unlocked door opened on well-greased hinges. Aether lights hung from the ceiling, extended the deathly light across the entryway. A stairway traveled up alongside a hallway that lead further into the first floor.

He followed the hallway and found it ended at two doors to each side. The door on the left was unlocked so he opened it and took a quick look inside. The cluttered workshop proved much more elaborate than his meager bench had been. In the far corner was a lab table with bubbling beakers heated by blue flames. Across from the door he found a workbench with a medium sized automaton lying on it. A dim blue glow shone out its open chest.

He didn't hear the door behind him open, didn't notice anyone there until he was almost knocked to the floor by a man shorter than himself. He recovered faster than the other. The man, still oblivious to Tisdan, mumbled something about cleaning women and equipment where it didn't belong.

Tisdan relaxed, his breath released in a quiet sight, watched the man dust himself off for a minute. "Um, Hello?"

He looked around and then focused on Tisdan for the first time. "How did you get in here?"

"The door was open?" This couldn't be the shaper Jak had sent him too. Something about him ground against Tisdan's intuition. He must have missed something.

"Oh right," he stepped toward the work bench. He left Tisdan in the doorway without a second glance.

"I was hoping you might be able to help me."

"The way out is the reverse of the way you came in." He grabbed a wrench and struggled with a bolt around the automatons midsection.

"Jaktor said you might be able to tell me something about this." Tisdan moved to the work bench as he pulled the amulet out of his waist-sash.

He dropped the wrench onto the workbench and looked again at Tisdan. As his eyes dropped to the amulet in his hand, the man's eyebrows scrunched together and he gave a slight jerk of his jaw. "What's this then." He drew a magnifying glass from his tool box and stepped around the bench to get a closer look. He held the amulet with tongs as he examined both sides through the magnifier. After a few minutes on each side he voiced a "hhhmmm," before he stepped back around to the other side of the workbench. The blue glow grew dimmed the further it moved away from Tisdan. He moved it closer and further away from Tisdan as the glow changed with its proximity. "It would seem that it has attuned to you. Give me your hand."

"Why?" Tisdan stepped back.

"Stop the shenanigans and give me your hand." His voice had taken an icy chill as he swiped at Tisdan's hand.

Tisdan offered his left hand, the hand that had been holding the amulet. The amulet's glow highlighted the deep indentations in Tisdan's fingertips. He had felt nothing other than the throbbing pain in his thumb that grew stronger with the amulet in the shaper's hand.

The shaper guided him closer to the light. The glyphs from the amulet had embedded themselves across his fingertips, though he only felt the sensation on his thumb. He needed the amulet back. A part of him had gone missing even as he knew where he could find it.

The shaper examined the markings on Tisdan's fingers with the magnifying glass. "This is most unusual. How long has this been in your possession?" He set the amulet on the work bench. The amulet inched toward Tisdan's hand, moved with a life of its own back to its home.

"This is an area outside of my study." With a sheet of paper and charcoal, the shaper traced the glyphs embedded in Tisdan's fingertips. He raised an eyebrow and made a tsk noise. Using the tongs to grasp the amulet he examined the markings on its surface and compared them to the charcoal outlines. "The markings are similar to ones I have seen, but the variations are troubling. The order these appear in seems of importance as well. You must tell me how you came about this, where is the source."

"There was a man in the market this morning." Tisdan slipped the amulet back into his sash. "It was only by happenstance. I needed the coins."

"Surely not a beggar. No this would not be something given to a beggar."

"It was in his purse, along with some silver." Sweat began to bead at his brow. "I only wanted the coins."

The shaper stood up and went to the wash basin near the lab equipment. He filled a couple glasses with water. When he came back to the work bench he offered one to Tisdan.

"This isn't shaper magic. I am not sure what this is really," he caught Tisdan's eye. "But it interests me."

Tisdan looked intently at his fingertips. They had taken on the glow of the amulet. He had felt no pain but the scaring was unmistakable. "How can we find out what this is?"

"I have a couple tests we can run. The real challenge and help would be to find who this came from. If we knew that we might have a bit more to work with."

"It happened so fast. The only thing I really remember was he was large." He looked at the automotan body lying on the slab. "He was in a hurry, but it was morning. Many people rushing around, especially on market day."

The shaper stood up then rummaged around in the storage space behind the work bench. Rooting with a purpose, he left no tool unturned. "A ha!" He pulled out an odd-looking helmet. At the front was a lens and the sides had ear coverings. The majority of the system was brass plates connected by what appeared to be glass tubes. He looked at Tisdan's head and then made some quick adjustments to the contraption. "This should help."

Raised eyebrows as Tisdan looked at the contraption, "What, is that?"

"A memory transducer," He looked at Tisdan with a full smile. "I have been working on it for some time now. It should work perfectly for our purposes here."

"What do you propose?"

He moved closer to Tisdan. "The way it works is, you wear it like this," He mimed putting it over his head with the lens at his forehead. "As I ask you questions about the incident, this lens will project your memories onto the wall, here."

"And this works?" Tisdan shifted slightly in his seat. Clearing his throat, "What will happen to me?"

"Theoretically nothing." He adjusted another knob on the apparatus. "I have not noticed any ill effects on my test subjects anyway."

"What test subjects?"

"I have been working at the sanitarium trying to understand some of the inmates that have not been influenced into complete madness."

"I don't find this very reassuring."

"Don't be a baby." He quickly removed Tisdan's bowler hat and placed the contraption in its place. Another adjustment shocked Tisdan into a rigid sitting position. "That should do it."

The amulet was in Tisdan's hand again as the shaper turned away to connect wiring to a control panel beside the work bench. A light pressure began to build in his hand. A gentle pulse that he knew came from the amulet. Closing his eyes, he focused on the pulse.

Images flitted through his mind. He saw the morning again; like he was still there. The fat man pushed through the crowd, paying little attention to those around him. Spying the weight of the coin purse, Tisdan saw an easy mark, distracted and harried. It had been nothing to do a quick bump and grab, but he did not expect the reaction from the mark.

He felt neither the pouch in his hand nor the dagger that came from the belt he had bumped into. He saw it all as a spectator. Though it meant little to him still. The kill had been easy and it shocked him at how little he felt from it.

A sharp jolt Brought him back to the present. The shaper grumbled under his breath as he fussed over the crystals on the panel. He picked up a wrench and smacked it down on a plunger attached to one of the wires coming from Tisdan's new headdress.

"Are you sure this is going to work?" Tisdan poked at him with a yard stick he found on the workbench.

The shaper turned from the panel to look at Tisdan, his brow creased in concentration. His eyes grew wide and he turned toward the wall. An eerie glow emanated from the head gear and projected to the wall. The face of the fat man grew in clarity as it focused within the glow. "It appears that something is working..."

He turned back to Tisdan. "I have seen him before, a scribe within the magistrate's office. At least he was." Realization hit him hard. "This is bad, really bad."

"What do you mean?"

He pulled the device from Tisdan's head unceremoniously, then attempted to help him from his stool. ""It was you, wasn't it? You need to get out of here. I can't be found with you."

Tisdan pushed him into the control panel "This isn't the first time today I've been pushed around because of this amulet. But it's going to be the last. What's going on?"

The shaper stomped hard on Tisdan's foot, then pushed away. Small and quick worked to his advantage in most circumstances. But Tisdan had training and was determined to keep the upper hand. Tisdan grabbed the shaper by his collar as he tried to squeeze by him.

Their struggle knocked a set of shelves down on top of Tisdan and the shaper. A couple of vials burst as they hit the ground sending putrid gases into the air. Both gagged and retched with tear filled eyes as they pushed the shelves away and as one, rushed to the door.

The beginnings of fire had made its way up the side of the work bench and lab table. At the door, the shaper slipped on a coat as he passed through. Tisdan caught a feint outline as the coat engulfed him and he disappeared.

He stepped onto the street as a minor explosion rocked the building. Across the street, Tisdan turned back to see smoke billow out the second story windows. The shaper was nowhere to be seen.

Something about the amulet had caused a stir but he was no closer to figuring it out. He walked in the general direction of the train station and then back to Jak's. At least there he could catch some sleep and figure out his options in the morning.

The chill of the night air Brought a fog with it. The billowy mass filled the area around him so fast that the buildings on each side of the street turned to mist. Cold, alone, the only light he could see came from his hand and the amulet he grasped. The pulse of blue light gave him just enough illumination to see the area directly in front of him and Tisdan used it to guide him along the street toward the stations.

The trip, a short few blocks away, had taken a turn unexpected. In the distance, howls filled the night air, the baying of hounds on the hunt. A cold chill crept from his hand, down his arm, and gripped his spine. But he soldiered on. The station wouldn't that much further, just one foot and the next. He forced himself forward, the hidden world around him gave him a little solace.

The howls came again, closer this time. Their voices came from three directions around him. And again, closer still. The beasts pushed him forward, away from their cries. He wanted to run, to escape the beasts but he knew it wouldn't be enough. He could feel it deep in his bones that the only way to break free of their hunt was to leave. The words had come into his mind and he knew them to be right but even then, he couldn't understand what they meant.

Tisdan stepped through the mists back on the street, but not where he had started. He knew the neighborhood. He had traveled from hightown to midtown, a block away from Jak's apartment. Bright burning street lamps illuminated the empty streets around him.

The amulet no longer glowed. He slipped it back into his sash as the fog was cleared around him. He jogged to Jak's place the last of the night chill left him as vapor in the run. Tisdan's steady breath and thump of his feet on the road were the only sounds to greet him. The hounds in the mist had become little more than a memory.

The door to Jak's apartment was open just as his had been, the lock sliced clean through. Inside, the apartment was shrouded in darkness. He pulled the amulet from his sash and willed it to light. Strange shadows danced with its bluish glow.

The apartment had been ransacked. He found Jak in the training room, what was left of him anyway. His body had been broken and battered, cold and dead. The fingers from his right hand were missing. By the look of it, they had been pulled from their sockets, torn from the stump of his hand. Cuts and bruises covered his upper body and his head hung loose at an odd angle, no longer attached to his spine.

He carried what was left of the man to his bed. Though it wasn't much the thought of leaving him like he had found him was unbearable. He had never been a religious man but he did his best to say a few words before he closed the bedroom door, closed himself from the memories of Jak when he had still been alive.

Tisdan weighed his options. He could stay here for a bit longer, the damage in their search had already been done. But he couldn't bear the thought of sharing the space with the memories, and with the dead. He felt like an intruder, an interloper in a mausoleum.

As he sat in the living room a glass vodka in hand, his final salute to his friend, he remembered the extra work Jak had done to the building. Jak had built in an escape route that would still be hidden. A trap covered a tunnel that led to a building on a street away from this one. If he was quick and quiet he could make it there and slip away without being found.

The rug was still in place, though covered now by a chair. He pushed the chair aside and lifted the door, giving himself enough room to slip out and shut the door again. The rug would stay in place keeping the door hidden.

The amulet gave him enough light to see the path. Cold, rough, earth comprised the walls. The passage had been built for Jak, giving Tisdan some clearance. Though it was tight, there was enough room to move comfortably. The tunnel itself was straight. It went directly to the next building without side tunnels. He was at the exit in just a few minutes.

He still couldn't believe what he had seen. Jak was good, beyond belief good. That was one of the reasons Tisdan had been studying with him. Whatever had gotten the drop on him and torn him up like that, that was something Tisdan didn't want to come across.

How it had found Jak in the first place was a mystery. He assumed that it was a search for him and Jak was caught in the search. Jak must have died trying to protect him. Betrayal wasn't out of the question but still, he liked to think that he and Jak were more like brothers. Brothers don't turn on brothers.

He stepped into the room just outside the tunnel. Another trap-door covered by a rug was the egress from the tunnel. The room was empty. The rug covering the tunnel looked out of place. Opening the trapdoor and moving the rug had kicked up dust, though around the room it had settled in a thick blanket. His footprints would be obvious when he left the place.

The amulet's glow shone bright into the next room. Layers of persistent dust buried the stack upon stack of boxes. So many boxes filled the room that the exit remained lost in the maze.

With a small effort, he willed the amulet to grow dark again, then slipped it back into his sash. For a moment, his mind lingered on the power he had within the amulet. A power he shut down, but at the same time he felt more, something ready to surge out of him.

The boxes had been stacked in neat rows, easier to navigate than he had expected, even in the dark. The one path through the room did not lead directly to the exit door. His steps twisted and wound across the floor.

Images of Jak flooded his mind as he shambled through the room. Broken, beaten, his life gone and there had been nothing he could have done about it. The exit door ahead of him pushed the thoughts from his mind. He took a deep breath and held it, then pushed the door open. A quick blast of cold night air washed across his face.

Fog surrounded him, a mist like before he arrived at Jak's. The disorientation he had felt before had slipped away, but this did not reassure him. Already he could hear the distant howls and knew they would come for him. With a steady breath, he centered himself and then ran, ran deeper into the mist.

Talons scraped against a pavement he could not quite feel under his feet. The beasts were close, so very close. They had anticipated his return and waited for him. He had no time to think, little room to breathe. He pushed himself away from the beasts that chased him in the fog, the gentle drum beat amulet power in his hand driving his pace.

He never saw them, though he felt their presence. The creatures of the mist drove him as they growled and yipped in the obscuring mist. They limited the directions he could run, though they never quite came into view. After what felt like an age of running through the shrouded night he realized that it was more than just the creatures of the mist that had guided him, images had flashed in his mind, thoughts of safety, thoughts of home.

With the realization, the mist had cleared around him as well. Still he ran, and tumbled to a halt when he twisted mid stride to run toward his apartment building.

The apartment was just as he had left it, ransacked and gutted. No one had claimed his space or removed anything he had left. He wasn't sure how he would secure the door again, though locks seemed to pose no challenge for what was looking for him.

A flash came into his mind, indistinct, shimmery. A glimmer of an idea. He gave a sidelong glance to the amulet. Its glow provided no answers. He wasn't sure what it meant but he felt an urge to place a hand on the door handle.

He grasped the cold metal and the glow of the amulet dimmed. A wave of energy traveled from the amulet up his arm, through his chest, and then down the other arm to the door handle. There was no light, no swirling colors, just a wave of energy. It lasted for a brief moment and then was gone. The door was shut tight. So tight he could not open it when he leaned away pulling the handle. Locked in his room, he cleared debris away from his bed of straw. He was asleep before his head hit the pillow.

Dreams of wolves haunted him. Creatures that hunted with claws to rip and tear. Their howls reverberated through his mind. All through his dreams, his fears, a soft blue glow caressed him and the world around him. He woke with a start when a giant wolf beast had reached for him, and caught its talons into the flesh of his arm.

His room had been suffused with a blue glow and his left forearm ached like it had been through a shredder. There were tears in the flesh, crusted over and scarred, damage that hadn't been there the night before. He held the medallion, and for a moment felt that it had fused to the flesh of his hand.

Tisdan wiggled his fingers to assure himself he could release it. They had cramped during the night, clasped tight against the medallion. It was an effort of will to straighten his fingers again.

As he sifted through his pockets, he remembered the man from the train. The card. The man had given him a card to get a hold of him. There would be no payment, that was a given. At least not something he would be able to spend. He would be lucky to come away with his life.

It seemed like an ordinary card at first glance. Monsignor Brackstone 438 Sycamore Lane, a high-town address. A small emerald stone had been embedded in the upper left corner of the card. The words shifted and shimmered with varied colors, shaper magic.

He had slept longer than he originally thought. It was approaching late afternoon, and the sun neared the end of its journey across the sky. With Jak gone his options were limited. It was a fool's errand but his path decided, and the station was close.

Later in the day the stations would slow down to pick back up again when workers returned for the evening. The crowd wasn't such that Tisdan would be able to blend in and find a hidden way onto a train.

A cheap seat to high-town ran 3 copper. His money pouch was light but he still had the gold coin from the girl. This would buy him a good meal and more than a few trips to high town. He hated to spend it, gold in low-town would draw more attention than he wanted or needed. He paid for a private cabin like he did it all the time.

He settled in for the long ride to high-town. The amulet was back in his hand again. He hadn't taken the time to examine it since the time at the shaper's lab and that had been a brief glance.

The glow he used as a light seemed to come to him on instinct alone. He wasn't sure how he did it though it felt natural. In the shaper's lab it had spoken to him. What else could it have been? That image on the wall, the amulet showed him what had happened though his recollection had been cloudy at best. The door at his place had been another moment when the amulet responded to him. His need for safety jammed the door into place.

But none of this told him anything about the amulet itself. And then the mist, that strange mist that crossed the miles of the city. The amulet was something more than just the metal and its inscriptions.

Lost in thought, he didn't hear the knock at the door. The second knock startled him, woke him from his reverie. He expected the conductor, waiting for his ticket or payment. It was the girl from yesterday.

"Ticket please?" Her soft smile burned through him as she pushed past him into the cabin. She glanced at the benches before she gave him a nod. "Do you often find yourself speechless?" she asked.

He stood in the open door, his mouth agape. It took him a few moments to collect his thoughts again. "Have we met?" The words felt hollow, as he stumbled over better responses in his mind. He lost the fleeting thoughts as he shut the door then sat on the bench across from her.

"It was only yesterday," she said. "Do you woo so many girls that I am so easily forgotten?"

He readjusted his sash, ensuring the amulet was still in its place. "Did we have dinner?" He gave her a wry smile. "I know, we had tea at Donovan's last week. You spilled jam on your dress."

She frowned at him, crossing her arms. "Now you are simply toying with me," she said. "And to think I found you to be a proper gentleman when last we conversed."

"I remember now, it was on the train. We shared a car before." His smile was softer, warmer.

She leaned forward, closer to him. "Much better. You left me at midtown. I had hoped to spend more time in your company."

"I have business in high-town today."

"Really? How long will you stay?" she asked. "We must have dinner. You will have time for dinner?"

"I can make time," he said. "But I... I don't even know your name."

"It is settled then. We shall have dinner at, Donovan's." She smiled her eyes locked on his as she offered her hand. "Jillian."

They continued with light conversation until the trained pulled into the high-town station. The conductor never knocked on their door.

They were the last to disembark, jostled through a group coming on. They stepped out into the chill, early evening air. Outside the station they walked to the street her arm in his.

"Are you sure I am dressed for Donovan's?" he asked.

Her gaze settled on his eyes. "You'll be fine," she said. "If I didn't know better, I would think you are trying to run out on me."

He didn't answer her, his attention pulled away to the cab that stopped at their section of the of the roadway.

"You aren't planning on running out on me, are you?" she asked.

He held her hand and answered, "Not at all, but I do have some business I need to attend to."

"Pish," she said. "Men and their business. That can wait, we'll have dinner first."

He held the door for her, watched as she stepped into the cab. Tisdan stood at the door unsure if he should follow, caught by his own inaction. She took his hand from the door and gave a gentle tug.

"You won't be getting away so easily this time," she said. The door shut as the cab pulled away from the curb. "You aren't often taken to dinner, are you?"

"To be honest," he said. "This is not something that happens, not to me. I eat on the go quite a bit."

"An apple from the stands does not count as proper dinner," she said.

His attention came back to her. "Apples are a rare treat," he said. "They are better than the meat pies that Lau Bay sells."

"I have never experienced one of these," she said. "Is this "Lau Bay" a restaurant?"

"Nah, he sells at a stand on market day. His meat pies are awful but some call them filling."

She digested the information, as her gaze never left him. "There is so much of your world I don't know," she said. "One day you shall have to show me around." Her cheeks flushed red as she turned away from him with a soft giggle.

The cab pulled up to the curb outside of an old building. The bright sign, the word Donavan's written in aether light, illuminated the walk to the door. A doorman, dressed in a deep red uniform jacket, stood immobile beside the entrance.

Jillian took Tisdan's hand. "He's with me."

The doorman looked her over, then stepped aside. He said nothing as they walked through the door.

"You make it look easy," Tisdan said.

She smiled, that same smile she gave him on the train, then whispered, "They know me here."

Benches with soft cushions lined one wall, next to a staircase leading to an upper floor. The staircase had an ornate railing made from dark stained oak. The light for the room came from frosted glass sconces along both walls while leading to the upper floor as well. She guided him to the door at the far end of the entryway.

Light flared through the doorway when she pulled it open. A blast of light that glared at them as new wonders caught his eyes from every direction. Crystal chandeliers hung from the ceiling. Open tables were spread throughout the room with diners in various stages of dinner. But these were not what drew his attention. Instead the private tables scattered throughout cut a different picture of the setting. All that could be seen were the screens. Divider walls surrounded several tables within the dining room. The light from above diffused and fell away from the top of each island. Those inside had complete privacy from the world outside.

"Now I know I am not dressed for this," Tisdan said.

She pulled him into the room with her, and twined her arm into his. "I have a standing table," she said. "We never need reservations." They stopped at a table with settings for 6. "I can get us something more intimate if you prefer."

He felt the eyes of the other patrons burning into him. A naked feeling that he couldn't shrug away. When he glanced around the room, no one looked in their direction, but he couldn't shake the feeling. His entire body had tensed with anticipation of ... something, something he couldn't quite explain. "It might be best. I feel a bit exposed here," he said.

Jillian spoke with a waiter before they went to the table. Tisdan held her chair before sitting himself. Moments after they sat down a small crew rushed into place setting up screen walls around the table closing them in to an intimate space. The only opening, aside from overhead, was a doorway to allow serving staff access.

The light in their intimate space became softer, the glow of several candles. The screens had created a shroud cutting them off from the light of the chandeliers. Tisdan hadn't noticed it at first but their table had shrunk as well. Instead of service for six the table had become smaller, more intimate. There were now only settings for two. There was still space enough to move around if need be but it felt as if the restaurant had become a space devoted solely to them.

A waiter filled their white wine glasses, first Jillian's and then Tisdan's. He placed the wine bottle in an ice bucket beside the table then exited the room without a word.

Jillian traced her finger across the rim of her glass, her eyes on Tisdan. "Is something wrong?"

"What just happened?"

"I mentioned that we would like some privacy."

The interplay of the light in the golden liquid caught Tisdan's eye as he raised the glass. He took a sip savoring the oak that mingled with the soft fruits. As he set the glass to the table a new flavor caught him in the wine's finish. For a moment, the world around him stopped as his breath caught in his lungs.

"La Troit de Cirous," she said. "It is one of the best whites on their list. I have a few bottles reserved for me and special guests. Do you like it?"

"I have never tasted anything quite like it," he said.

The waiter returned with small plates of food. Small pink bodies in a creamy white sauce. Jillian called them prawns and mentioned that they came from the sea. He had never been to the sea, the street foods he knew masked their origin in mixtures and questionable sauces. The dinner progressed much the same, dishes were cleared away and something new was set before him. A new wine or beer set out for each course, something that went with each dish to complement and enhance the meal.

Dinner ended, its final course a chocolate torte with champagne. He looked down on it, pressing his fork against it at different angles. "What is the best way to go about this?" he asked.

"Small bites, letting each one melt against your tongue," she said. "Chocolate is something to be savored." She cut into hers with her fork, brought it to her mouth, and then sipped her champagne. Her eyes closed as the chocolate and champagne joined between her lips.

"I never knew food could be such an adventure," he said.

"There are many adventures you do not yet know about." The words came out of nowhere, but Tisdan knew the voice, had heard it before. It broke through their solitude, disrupting the illusion of privacy. He stepped into the light, as their table grew to accommodate him. The man from the train, dressed much the same as the time Tisdan met him, placed silk gloves beside the table setting in front of him.

"Daddy," she said. "I wondered if you might come to dinner tonight."

"Daddy?" Tisdan asked. "What's going on here?"

"I would think it obvious," he said. "My daughter is having dinner with you."

Tisdan stood up knocking his chair down in his haste. The monsignor's hand caught his wrist as he stepped away from the table.

"Sit, enjoy your dessert," he said. "The torte here is the best you will find in the world."

Tisdan righted his chair and then sat. But he did not bring himself into the light of the table. "This was a set up," he said to Jillian. "I should have known."

"What is he talking about?" she asked.

The monsignor held a glass of dark ruby liquid to his nose, inhaled its aroma. He savored the flavors before he answered. "Business, my dear. Your young friend has an item my employer is interested in."

"I have no clue what you're talking about," Tisdan said.

"Daddy is a collector," she said. "They find lost items and bring them back to where they belong." She paused for breath, holding Tisdan's eyes with her own, "What have you done?"

The monsignor said, "No one has done anything. Your young friend here, stumbled across something recently that I am trying to bring back to its proper owner."

His smug smile made Tisdan's skin crawl. He didn't want to cause a scene and upset Jillian. The concern he saw in her eyes calmed him. "This has become just a bit too much for me," he said. "I am grateful for the hospitality Miss Jillian, but I think it's time I to go." He dodged the monsignor's hand as he reached to hold Tisdan back again.

Tisdan was through the doorway and into the main dining room without looking back.

The dining room had cleared out, though the chandeliers were still lit, their light had dimmed. A few staff remained in the room to clear the tables and clean. None of them paid attention to him as he made his way to the door.

He chanced a last look back into the dining room. No one followed him. Jillian and her father were nowhere to be seen. He went through the door and back into the night air.

Deserted streets and no cabs, he traveled on foot, through an area he didn't know. The chill night air cut deep through his jacket and shadows twisted and swirled through the deathly light of the aether lamps. The moon had hidden behind clouds and left only the lamplight, to guide him.

Without a thought he held the amulet, guided by a pull, a need to change direction. Tisdan held the address on the Monsignor's card in his mind, though he didn't know where to find it. Dull vibrations carried images to his mind, places he did not recognize until he came upon them as he drove himself forward. It spoke to him in a rudimentary manner, messages that had become easier for him to understand. Markers looked the same from block to block, little to help him discern where he was in relation to few parts of high-town he knew.

After a few blocks of what felt like forced wandering a cab passed him and then pulled up to the side of the street ahead of him. The passenger stepped out of the cab and beckoned for him. Though shadows obscured her features, he knew her. She had been alone in the cab.

"Where is your father?"

"I am sorry," she said. "I didn't know anything about this." She stopped a short distance away. "I enjoyed our conversation and only wanted to continue."

He cupped the amulet shrouding its light with his hand. "Why should I believe you?" he asked. "It seems convenient that the daughter of a man I briefly met is now interested in conversation."

"We need to get off the streets," she said. Wrinkles creased the bridge of her nose as she glanced past him, further down the street. She pulled the edge of her wrap tight to her chest. "Quickly."

The hairs at the back of his neck turned prickly, but it wasn't because of her. He felt something in the air that he hadn't felt before. It was distant though coming up behind him. "Fine, I am tired of walking anyway."

The cab's door snapped shut with a soft click, and cut off the sounds of the night. Oppressive solitude filled the air around them. Tisdan cleared his throat to an echo he hadn't expected in so tight a space. "What's going on?" He said. His voice boomed in his ears.

"Home," she said. The cab pulled away from the curb. "I don't live with my father. I rarely even see him." She sat back in her seat, though she inclined toward him.

"That doesn't answer my question," he said. "What part is it you play in all this? Why should you even care?"

"I saw what happened," she said. "I was probably the only person to see the whole thing."

He paused as the words traveled through his mind. Images of the fat man and the knife in the back of his neck haunted him. The skin of his arms prickled with the goose flesh of a chill. "I never meant for it to happen. I'm not a killer."

"I saw it all. But there's more to the story," she said.

He was ready to bolt, but to where? There was nowhere left for him to run and she would find him anyway or her father would. He still didn't know which of the two would be the worse situation. "What do you want from me?"

"The amulet comes to mind," she said. "But I think it may be too late for that now. You don't know what it is you have, do you? It was just a day at the market for you?"

Trust in low-town wasn't something that you could afford. Trust got you killed or worse. He lived alone and survived alone. Jak had been the closest thing to a friend, but that was more of a business arrangement. Jak was gone, he had nothing left.

"I'm a thief, always have been. You do what you need to do to survive."

"I don't care," she said. "Your life before now means nothing to me. If the amulet hadn't come into your possession, we wouldn't be speaking." She leaned back in the seat, cushioned by pillows. Her eyes did not leave his face.

Drawn to her eyes, he could drown in their depths. "At least I know where I stand," he said. "What's changed? You could just kill me and take it. It isn't like you haven't killed before." It was a gamble; he wanted to trap her into a confession. He hoped she hadn't killed Jak, but anything was possible.

"The amulet has bonded to you. Though I'm not sure why. I don't think my father knows this yet."

The carriage turned down a dark street, ending in a cull de sac. There were only a few houses, the carriage stopped at the one at the end of the street. The house covered two lots, with space and yard separating the houses on either side of it. It wasn't a mansion but, like many of the homes in high-town it was much larger, than you would find in other parts of the city. The buildings in low-town had been broken into many different units within the larger buildings. The homes in high-town were just as big but each one owned by only a single family or individual.

When the carriage stopped, he stepped out first then helped her get out as well. The door opened before she touched it, lights came on when they crossed the thresh hold. Power through the aether was at work, though she wore no visible gems. The house expected her and responded to her presence.

Tisdan followed her lead through the entryway and then further into the home. Rich woods inlaid with gems and crystals of different sizes and colors marked their passage through the hall. Lights pulsed to life before they were needed. They hovered and from nowhere and everywhere at once. She motioned for him to step ahead of her into a sitting room. One wall had book shelves that extended from the floor to the ceiling. Off to the side was a bar, ten feet long with a few stools in front of it. The center of the room had two couches and two wing back chairs with matching ottomans. Piles of papers covered a large oaken desk placed in front of floor to ceiling windows.

He felt a need to go to the desk and dig through its papers. He had always had a strong instinct to guide him but this was something more. A pull at his body beyond conscious thought. He fought against himself to maintain his composure.

"Make yourself at home," she said as she stopped behind the bar. Clinking glassware belied her hands hidden by the wooden counter.

He went to the window, his view lost to the darkness outside. For him, it was an excuse, a chance to move closer to the desk without appearing to do so. "I imagine it's a great view."

"Yeah. I forget about it most of the time." Her voice felt distant, distracted as she worked behind the bar.

The papers on the desk were a jumble, little in the top layer he could make sense of. The feeling drew him to the desk, told him what he sought would be found deeper, within the stacks themselves.

Jillian nudged him with her elbow, and knocked him back into the moment. "A night cap," she said as she swirled the amber liquid to release its heady aroma. "Relax, you're safe here." She moved to the couches motioning for him to follow.

He sat in one of the chairs, facing her on the couch. The distance gave him comfort, a safety net. Part of him remained at the desk.

She watched him, a slight smile at the corners of her mouth. "They don't know what it can do yet," she said. "The amulet, the runes on it aren't shaper magic."

He said nothing. The amulet remained in his sash. It's presence had become a part of him. It's pull to search the desk scratched at the corners of his mind.

"It was coming to me," she said. "The scribe was on his way to me, so I could get it out of the city."

This was something he hadn't expected. He forced himself to remain blank and calm. "That day on the train, you knew I had it?"

She no longer looked at him, her thoughts turned to the past. "He had discovered something about the amulet, something he was unwilling to let fall into shaper hands." She took a long drink from her glass and finished it off. "Do you know how shaper magic works?" Her attention returned to him with physical weight.

"I know it has something to do with the crystals," he said.

"They need a focus. The crystals enhance and focus the aether." She stood and walked to the bar. "The shapers control their power by control of the crystals. Only they have access to them." She poured brown liquid into her glass.

"What does this have to do with the amulet?" He shouldn't have asked it. He mentally chided himself for saying too much. He was drawn into the story and didn't like it.

"It's a key," she said. "Only a couple people know this. It can open the aether." With her drink in hand she sat down on the couch facing him. She considered his eyes, expectant, waiting. When he said nothing, she pushed on. "It's believed it frees the wielder from the need of the crystals."

"I don't understand," he said. "What does that mean?"

"Shaping without the crystals, means that there would be no controls over what the shapers could or would do. Their power would grow with nothing to stop it, at least for one shaper." She paused with a deep breath before she continued. "With nothing to hold them back they would use their power with abandon. The crystals keep them in check."

"And they would do anything to get it back?" he asked. "This doesn't tell me what part you play in all this?"

"What's your intention with amulet?"

He stood up, the amulet in his hand. Its blue fire shone brighter than the aether lights in the room. "It is mine. It is a part of me."

She did not move, transfixed by the glow. "Do you control it? Or is it controlling you?"

He looked down on her; she was small, frail. She would be broken easily. She would break, faster even than the assassin. She did not have his training. A small voice in his head came through. Stop. Enough. She does not have to die. The glow from the amulet tapered off. He could hear his own voice in his head. An inner battle of crashing waves between himself and the other voice. And then a light, calming, soothing him back to himself.

She stood next to him, taking his free hand into her own. "The amulet has its own agenda. It wasn't chance that you stole it. It wanted you to find it." She stroked his hand soothing him, pulling him from the edge. "It is becoming a part of you, but at what cost?"

"I killed him," he said. His eyes, his vision lost to the distance. He saw the battle with Jak, the clarity of truth breaking through the clouds in his mind. Jak took him in and helped him. He killed him without even a thought. Broke him with his hands, snapped his neck and his back as if they were twigs. All the while the blue glow had filled him.

"We can fix this," she said. Her words pulled him back into the room. "I can free you. This doesn't have to control you anymore."

"I don't think there is time left to fix this. I have lost which voice is mine and which is the amulet." Even as he said it, he felt a distance from the moment. A separation between him and his body as he looked down on the room from above.

"I brought you back. I know what it can do." She walked over to a cabinet on the wall and pulled out a few trinkets. "Put the amulet away for a moment."

He returned it to his sash. She slid a ring onto his ring finger. The ring had a band of red crystal inlaid through the middle of the circular band. It began to glow with an incandescent red light as she whispered soft words into it. The light faded with the warmth of her breath on his fingers.

"This will only work for a little while, if at all." She looked into his eyes without humility. She was expectant, waiting for his response.

He could no longer feel the heartbeat of the amulet. A part of him was now missing, an empty house with a dead body in it. His mind was quiet and still, while screaming at the same time. And then it hit, like a bandage had been torn from an open wound. Searing pain knocked him to his knees. He could not move, could barely breath. His vision had become a red blur. Pain filled his body past the breaking point. He fell to the floor, unable to move.

She stepped over his body and pulled the amulet out of his sash with a gloved hand. After dropping it into a pouch she stepped away from his body, her gloves falling at his waist. "Easier than I had expected," she said. She left the room, he remained on the floor where she had left him.

Time spent unconscious, drifted through a fuzzy realm where he had no idea where he was anymore. The pain, cut with indistinct voices, had been more than he could take. As the pain intensified his eyes cracked open. Chill, musty air filled his lungs. He had been moved.

Soft light in the distance broke the darkness. It crept around the edges of the door into the small room he woke in. His hands were bound behind him and a shackle bound his left ankle, its chain ended at the wall. It left little slack for movement.

He contorted his body into a sitting position then pushed against the wall and managed to stand. Through the struggle the blood rushed to his head. The room spun and the floor felt uneven as he fell back against the wall. Tisdan gulped in air as he fought to right his mind and perception to the world around him.

As his breathing settled and he adjusted to the space around him his mind flashed in panic. The ring. He twisted his hands across each of his fingers, all of them empty. With that he knew that the amulet had left him as well. It would be gone from his sash and now, maybe out of his life.

Jak had always told him to be prepared for anything. Forethought could get a prepared thief out of any situation and manacles were little more than practice for other locks. The manacles on his wrist had more play in them than he had expected. Not enough to break free, but they didn't pinch his wrists and he could maneuver. He slid down the wall, and brought his hands in front of him.

Long ago he had sewn a lock pick into the lining of his vest. He worked it free in short order and then twisted it through the locks of his manacles on his wrists and ankle.

He slipped back to its home before he felt around the room. Aside from the wall he had been chained to it seemed to be a simple ten by ten room. Wooden planking covered what would have been a dirt floor. The door to the next room, though closed, had not been locked.

Light in the next room had come from a sconce similar to the ones he had seen in Jillian's living room. A soft glow illuminated the base of the stairwell that rose like a walled tunnel to a closed door above. He stepped on the first stair and stopped. Something had changed. A twist in the air, a scrape of metal to wood, or maybe a smell. Something small that defied any logic had changed and stopped him in his tracks. Call it his survival instinct but something deep inside him screamed at him to go back.

Without another moment's hesitation, he swooped back to the place he had been chained. He snapped the manacle to his ankle as he heard voices at the top of the stairs. The scrape of the feet on the stairs masked the click as he snapped the manacles back on his wrists.

Light blasted into the room as they pushed the door open. The radiance blinded Tisdan for a moment as three dark shapes shuffled into the room. As his eyes adjusted he marked the forms of two brutes that stood to the side of the Monsignor. The gem at the top of the man's cane glowed with the bright light that had filled the room. It dimmed slightly as he poked Tisdan in the ribs with the end.

"Undo his ankle but not his wrists. We need him mobile but not free. I see you are awake," he said. "You have the choice to follow me on your own, or they will help you along. But either way you will be coming with me now."

"Where are we going?" Tisdan asked.

"That is of no concern to you at the moment. You should be more concerned with what happens if you do not do as I say."

"Rot in hell," he knew it was a mistake even before he finished the sentence. The thug on his left rabbit punched him in the side. The pain brought him to his knees.

"I have time," the Monsignor said. "Shall we continue?"

Tisdan stood up but did not look at him. The manacles on his wrists were clamped shut, though with enough space that he could free his hands in less than a heartbeat. All he needed to do was bide his time till the right opening presented itself.

"Take him upstairs."

The thugs each took an arm and frog marched him to the base of the stairs. He was then pushed up ahead of one while the other blocked his clear path to the door and possible freedom.

The top of the stairs led into the room where Jillian had trapped him. She was nowhere to be seen. Any trace that he had been in the room was gone. The thugs pushed him through the room then out the door.

Outside there was a horse drawn carriage. The cab of was covered with the curtains drawn. He did not have long to wonder what the inside would be like. The thugs shoved him in and barred the door on the outside.

The interior was spartan, wooden benches with no cushions. The curtains hid barred windows from those outside the carriage. He was not alone. Jillian lay on the bench across from him. Though she hid her face she could not hide the sobs that wracked her body.

Her hands were shackled as his had been. He wasn't sure if he should speak to her or let her continue. This could be another ploy. But they would already have the amulet. There was little else they could take from him now.

He slipped his hands free from the shackles and knelt beside her. "Why?" he asked.

She turned, her face puffy with red streaks from tears, as she struggled, flopping like a fish, to sit up. He lay a hand on her shoulder and then lifted her to a sitting position. "Thank you," she said, though she wouldn't look at him; her eyes focused to the ground at his feet.

The carriage jerked forward knocking him back onto the bench opposite Jillian. Tisdan moved on the bench so that he was across from her. "Why?" He asked it again. "Why did you do this?'

"The ring, it was only supposed to suppress the connection between you and the amulet," she said. "My father must have found it and changed the shaping." Her eyes had begun to water again as she spoke to him.

"They were waiting for us. I slipped the ring on your finger." She took a deep breath. "The shock hit me too. Not at first, but it dropped me just as you had fallen."

He said nothing, simply watched her. His eyes caught hers then dropped away again.

"I really was trying to help you. That thing is a power no one should have," she said. She adjusted herself on her bench, to find a comfortable position. "There is going to be a power shift. Damius will take over the council."

She dropped the name like he would know and understand who she spoke of. But like so many others outside of his world, it meant nothing. "You've never stepped into low-town," he said. "You talk about power shifts and politics, but you have never seen what these petty battles bring about." He was on his feet, at the door to the carriage. He pulled the curtain over the window aside and looked out over the dark street. "Every day, the people in low-town battle just for some bread. Your shapers have done nothing, nothing to help them."

She was quiet. The tears came again, though her body was not wracked with sobs. "You don't know what it's like," she said.

"I really don't care," he said. "You and your kind can have your petty wars. Go ahead kill each other. Just leave us out of it." The door was barred. He could not push it using his strength alone. He felt something, something he hadn't felt since the ring was placed on his finger. Power surged up through his left hand giving him a strength he hadn't known. The bar on the door, bent and broken, came away as the door flung open.

Tisdan, caught off guard could only stare at the empty space where the door had been. He looked back at Jillian and was about to jump out when she said, "Wait, take me with you." She came to her feet, though her hands were still bound. "I can help you still."

He pulled the lock pick from his vest, then removed her manacles. "Come with me or not, I don't care," he said. "But I'll leave you if you slow me down." He took one last look out the window then jumped out. He hit the ground in a roll absorbing the hit with his momentum. He had taken worse tumbles jumping from the trains.

Jillian looked out the open doorway, her eyes wide as the road slipped past. She jumped, more of a flop and roll, could have gone much worse than it did. A few scrapes, but nothing was broken or sprained. The carriage continued without them.

Tisdan helped her to her feet then dusted himself off. "Looks like we are in this together then," he said.

"How did you do that to the door?" she asked.

"Run."

She followed his gaze back to the carriage as it came to an abrupt stop. One of the thugs was at the door looking inside. The other tied up the horses and was coming toward them.

Tisdan didn't wait for her. He was half a block away when he turned his head to see if she was coming. She wasn't far behind but neither were the thugs. When Tisdan had a two-block lead on them they were still coming. He took Jillian's hand and turned down an alley. They were still at a full run when they came to the end. The thugs caught up, at the other end of the alley.

Panic climbed the edges of his thoughts, and he settled in to a technique Jak had taught him once. Tisdan closed his eyes and centered his attention on his breath, in and out. A center of calm pushed back the world around him as he let go of his fears

He shivered as fog began to form around him. It came in fast, too fast for natural fog. Jillian was still beside him. The thugs at the end of the alley blurred then faded away. He took Jillian's hand, squeezed it for reassurance. The building at their back grew fuzzy and indistinct, then was gone.

Still holding Jillian's hand, they walked through where the building had been. "What did you do?" Jillian asked.

"I didn't do it," he said.

"This is the aether, the place between," she said. "My father talked of traveling through here once."

"I think the amulet took me through here," he said.

They continued walking. The buildings around them had shapes in the fog but no substance. It took no effort for them to walk away from where they had been trapped.

"This isn't possible," she said. "People don't just step into the aether." They were blocks away from where they started. The fog was gone, but the night was still around them. They found solace in a different alley, hidden from the street.

"It just happens," he said. "I needed a way out and we made it out." He paced, a refusal to stand still.

"The only time I have seen a doorway, it took the power of the council to open it," she said. "Shapers don't travel through the aether."

"I'm not a shaper."

She grabbed him, a hand on each arm. "I don't think you grasp what is happening here. The amulet unlocked something in you." She was a few inches shorter than him, looking up into his eyes. "This is huge. This means that the amulet was something more than they even considered."

He pulled a glowing disc from his sash. "Well, then I guess it's a good thing they don't have it." He shoved it back into his sash.

She was taken aback, words didn't come to her. Her hands slid from his arms. "Wha...how..."

"I don't know," he said. "I felt it there after we left the fog. I think it has become a part of me, or maybe I'm a part of it."

"Do you realize what this means?" she asked, her arms flew wild while she talked. "They hoped to take its power for themselves. They will have no choice but to kill you."

"Um..." he began. "Why do they have to kill me?"

"To free the power." She stopped pacing. "Don't you get it. You remember how you got it?"

"You mean the fat man?" He looked off in the distance, lost in the memory. "I didn't mean to do that."

"Doesn't matter. The amulet found a new host," she said. "When they realize that the amulet is gone they won't be coming just to find it. They're coming to kill you."

"I don't like where this is going."

"We have to figure out how this thing works and fast," she said. "It's the only way you can defend yourself."

"I'm not going to defend myself. I'm taking the fight to them."

"You can't take on the whole council," she said.

"This isn't with the whole council," he said. "You said it yourself, your father is working for only one of them."

Tisdan fell to the ground, his chest heaving as he fought to catch his breath. He rolled to his back and turned to look at Jillian. "Set another one."

"You can't keep pushing like this," she said. "We'll have to move again at this rate." Her gaze had fallen back to the crystal in her hand as she searched herself for the strength to set up another trap.

They had been working like this for some time, moving from place to place to skirt around the searchers. All the while Tisdan fought through shaper magic to better understand the power that now filled him. The two were not the same, not for how they had found so far. Shaper magic could be called on at will. Jillian needed only the crystals to command the aether. Without them she lacked focus for her will.

His magic confounded everything she had learned growing up. It came from the subconscious. At first he had felt impulses, a guiding force to lead him where the magic would go. But as he continued to use it, something changed. It had become a reactive force within him that allowed him to create without thought. The magic was a part of him buried deep within his psyche. And she couldn't feel him.

Shaper magic left an imprint in the aether. The crystals carried a signature that other shapers could feel. The pulse of their crystals connected them through the aether. She knew when the searchers had found their locations, and Tisdan could shift them through the aether to a new cubby hole.

She pinned him in a wall of aether. Something she had used before. The force closed in tight around him and left him little space to move. Tisdan had been through exercises similar to this long ago, a lifetime ago, with Jak. Physical confines were not much different than being confined with aether. No difference at all with the tools to cut through either.

He closed his eyes as the force began to crush down on him. His thoughts settled on a single pin point of light, a piercing thought to focus his energy into a small section of the wall. After a moment energy flowed through him and a thin stream of power pushed back against the wall. As the energy scrambled it suddenly reformed and changed direction around him. He had just enough time to swing his body around and gain his feet. The power of the force that slammed into the ground where he had been left a dent in the dirt.

He rolled with it to stand. A glance her direction and she had relaxed her concentration to catch her breath. "Break?" He said. "We can afford a few minutes here."

Her nod, spoke volumes of how much work they had done. Her energy had been pushed further than she had ever thought possible. She opened her mouth to speak but found her voice had left her for the moment. Instead she rocked back on her heels and set the crystal down in front of her.

Tisdan scanned the small room they had holed up in. Part of a larger defunct factory they had a few neighbors in other parts of the building. They kept to themselves and the others had done the same. They weren't part of the group and didn't want to become any more visible than they were.

His mind hadn't stopped racing. Even with the push to learn his limits a part of him still thought ahead to where they would go next. She spoke the truth when she said they would have to move soon. Things hadn't changed for him, he had to keep moving.

"I think it's time," Jillian said. "We can't sit around all day wasting daylight." She picked up the crystal and took a deep breath. She released it in a slow exhale.

As a reflex he dropped into a crouch and opened his thoughts to the aether. And felt something else. The air around them had changed. Noises in the distance didn't account for the others they shared the space with. He couldn't place what it was but something different had entered their space. The hairs on the back of his neck stood on end as a chill raced down his spine.

"Did you hear that?" She stopped arranging the crystal pattern. "Something's not right."

He took a deep breath to calm himself. On its release he opened his senses, extended them beyond their room. It was there, just outside the door to their room. "Get ready," he whispered as he helped Jillian to her feet.

Something crashed against the door. Tisdan had jammed it closed with the power of the aether. The door shook in its frame something battered against a second time. On the third strike against the door, a beast crashed through the ceiling into their room.

Tisdan pushed Jillian behind him, to stand between the interloper and her. The hunched creature barely stood more than four foot. Though it wore clothes it had the visage of a beast, a snout with jagged teeth and tufts of fur grew in patches across its gnarled flesh. It growled from deep within its belly.

Tisdan pulled twin daggers from sheaths at the small of his back. A blue screen of energy formed in front of him. The air crackled in fits around the mass.

The creature's spring toward them stopped short by the shield of energy. It bounced off and spun in the air to land several feet away again. Another crash into the door rocked the frame and cracked its connection to the wall.

He glanced at the door and adjusted the energy shield's position. Tisdan pulled back, then threw a dagger at the beast with one fluid movement. The creature side stepped as the dagger whizzed by its head. "Any thoughts?" Tisdan asked.

"Close your eyes," Jillian said.

The crystal landed in front of the creature just as he clamped his eyes shut. A blinding flash burst around them, then plunged the room into darkness. Tisdan's eyes adjusted to the return to natural light as the creature flailed its arms, blinded by the flash.

Tisdan slipped behind the creature and drew his blade across its neck. It fell to the floor as the door suffered another slam. It wouldn't take another attack.

Tisdan retrieved his thrown dagger. He noticed a spot on the floor, cold sludge. The remains of the crystal, burned out in the blast of light.

"Bastads," she said. "They actually did it."

Her words brought him back. Tisdan called up the fog, a doorway into the aether and their escape from the other beasts outside their door.

"I can't believe they did it," Jillian said. She leaned against the window, her eyes unfocused on the world outside.

"What was that thing?" he said. After several quick trips, they had settled in a new location in midtown. Exhaustion had claimed them before they could consider another trip through the aether. So far, nothing had approached them.

She turned to face him, though she focused past him. "I heard rumors," she said. "I never believed them though. The whole thing is just... Well, it's wrong."

"Someone found a way to twist an animal with a person. I mean, what else could it be? You saw that thing, a beast twined, sculpted through crystals and aether into the form of a man." She shuddered and fell back against the wall. "I never thought they could, no, would do such a thing."

"I never saw it. But this isn't the first time I ran across one of these things," he said. "It was after I found the medallion, they had broken into my home. The claws, they ripped through metal and wood to get in."

Jillian paused as she focused on him, her gaze locked with his. "They aren't going to ask for it again. They intend to get it the same way you did."

"This thing leaves a trail of death in its wake." His gaze had fallen to the runes etched along the outer edge of the medallion.

Without warning a loud crash followed by an unearthly howl resounded from the floor below. They looked at each other and then for something to shore up their position.

They were exhausted, sick without sleep. Forever on the run with the creatures nipping at their heels the entire time. Only to realize what this had become. They were herded, like cattle. They were kept moving to this point, this confrontation.

"You can't run forever." The monsignor's voice boomed through the building. "Give yourselves up. We can free you of the burden." The crunch of sand and gravel could be heard as the Monsignor paced outside the building they were holed up in. "You are out of options," he said. "Jillian, you know there is nowhere else for the two of you to go. See reason."

"We can't just give up," she said. "Can't we walk one more time?"

Tisdan's body felt raw, his nerves aflame. "I don't think I can do it, not without a week in a bed first."

Jillian glanced down. The ring on her left hand had caught her attention. It had been a gift from her father long ago, an amber crystal that shone with a light glow when she thought of him. "It's me," she said. "You have to leave me."

Time slipped away from him. He had stepped outside of himself and now looked down at Jillian and his body still in the room. As he drifted higher the entire building came into focus. Every room that the beasts had broken through, and then the space where they might find solace.

"Leave me." She repeated, unaware of his vision. "They've been finding us through me." Tears cut a trail through the grime on her cheeks. "You stand a better chance without me weighing you down anyway."

"We can still get out of this," he said. He slid the rings off her fingers, and dropped them at their feet. "But we can't stay with any of this."

Through darkness, they followed the wall into a room deeper inside the building and a stairway that lead to an upper floor. He took her hand pulling her behind him. Nothing was said. Outside a room in the center of the hallway, he looked back for anything that followed them. They were there, a presence he couldn't escape from.

The room had suffered through time and neglect like the rest of the building. Crumbled walls and broken furniture were all that remained. Useless and broken, their purpose lost to the past. They stopped in the center of the room, hidden behind a wall of debris. The amulet was in his hand glowing blue. He held her left hand in his right hand, his eyes looking off in the distance.

There was no tingle, no feeling at all. For all she could tell they were still sitting on the floor with no change around them. "What did you do?" she asked.

"Hope," he said. A smile played at the corners of his mouth. "We might have a chance still. They were tracking us by your rings."

"Yeah," she said. "My father... He must have marked them. They were all I had left."

"They have been chasing your rings all this time. They can't sense the amulet. They can't sense me."

Something scraped the floor at the top of the stairs, the only sound they had heard for some time. His hand on her shoulder kept her down, close to him. Tisdan nodded toward the doorway with a finger to his lips.

They both jumped a little when the door to the room beside them had been broken through. And again when the room across from them had been torn into. The creatures weren't subtle. Clawing and growling they searched the rooms all through the floor.

But their room, Jillian realized too late, they hadn't closed the door. The creature came into the room, sniffing the air. It walked through the room, right past them without any recognition. With a last sniff of the air it left the room and moved on to the next.

"What just happened?" she whispered.

"I'm not sure how or why," he said. "But the amulet responds to my needs. We became one with the shadows. Nothing can find us right now."

They sat in silence, after the wolfen left their floor. The sky grew dark outside the window of the room they were in. Tisdan's muscles had grown cramped and sore from the time sitting on the floor. They refused to move or make any sound. It was only after several hours, well into the night that they finally felt safe to move. They had fallen asleep in each other's arms. They stretched and shook life back into numb muscles.

He put the amulet back into his sash before leaving the room to explore the damage to the rooms around them. The rooms that had closed doors had them torn from their hinges. The creature was thorough. It left nothing unturned in the rooms in its search for them.

"We can't keep doing this," Jillian said. "They were close this time. Our luck is going to run out."

They were on the first floor. Her rings had been taken from where they left them earlier. "Are there any other crystals on you that they could track?" he asked.

"That was it, I am completely out now," she said "I have nothing left to help you with."

"On my own," he said. "This is how it has always been." He reassured himself that his daggers and tools were in their proper places. "No sense spending any more time worrying about all this."

"What are you going to do?"

"The only thing we can do," he smiled, a smile that lingered as he faded away. "I am going to end this." His voice came from the shadows. The door to the street opened and then closed, a shadow lost in the darkness.

"Damn you," she said to the air. "What the hell am I supposed to do now?"

He hated leaving her. He'd spent so much time with Jillian that he felt a little off being on his own. There was a void he couldn't remember experiencing before she joined him. He felt a little guilty in the luxury of having her along. It was more than he had in the past.

Even with Jak, they had never spent much time together, not like this. Damn it, it was never supposed to happen like this. Jak, dead, gone by his hand. Jillian would survive, if he didn't do something crazy first. He hoped so, anyway. Neither of them had needed him. Until now he had thought he didn't really need them either. Too late for Jak though.

He hugged the shadows, invisible to prying eyes. Few trains ran in the middle of the night. Tired eyes wouldn't see him, wouldn't notice the shadow among others that boarded and melded into the back of a cabin. He slipped to the floor of a closet and leaned back against the wall with his eyes closed. Though he would be stiff from staying in the same spot for the trip he would be able to loosen up on his walk from the station.

They had gone over the location of the house daily, she wanted him to know exactly where he needed to go to find the shaper. He thought it odd but now that the decision had been made, it all seemed to fall into place. Take out the shaper, this Damius Arith. Cut them off at the source of his problems to get back to his life.

And that was the problem. He wasn't an assassin. He was a survivor. The few times he had taken life had been flukes, moments where he had left himself and the process had happened anyway. An unconscious decision made for him by outside forces. After each death, he had to run. Run to survive.

A calm came over him as he flipped the medallion front to back. He couldn't run anymore, wouldn't run anymore. Peace settled over him as he slid the medallion back into his sash. New energy filled him as his resolve grew. Today it would end.

He stepped out of the shadows as the train pulled into the station. He would walk in the open now. They couldn't take the amulet from him. He wasn't sure if they knew this yet, but it didn't matter. The only way that would happen meant his death. There were more ways to die than he originally thought.

The high-town station was all but deserted. A few passengers had left the train when he did. The station wasn't as big as the low-town station. Without the market and fewer travelers it wasn't a necessity.

He wouldn't be able to catch a cab, but he did know how to find the home he was looking for. He had some time to think as he walked. It was a double-edged sword, time to think. Seemed to him lately he hadn't had much time for that. His life was little more than survival mode. The amulet coming into his life didn't change that. Searching for what you need to survive versus fighting to survive, either way it was all about scraping by.

At one time he thought the shapers and those in high town had it so much better, in some places they did. But they were slaves to their shaping as much as he had been a slave to survival. He needed something more to break free of the chains that bound him. The amulet, he had realized, was something more than just a simple tool. It was a key, a key that opened a specific lock.

That was why it left the fat man. He knew little to nothing of what it could be used for. It found its way to Tisdan. Through happenstance it turned out he was a lock it could open. In the opening so much more became possible.

This time to think was the only thing in his life now that felt natural to him anymore. Before the amulet he had enjoyed his simple life in the station. From his perches, he could watch the lives of those coming and going. He was now pushed into something more.

He didn't notice the cab pull alongside him at first. It was quiet, blending into the night. It pulled ahead of him a short way and then stopped. The

Monsignor stepped out, stepped away from the cab but did not move toward Tisdan. "Chilly night for a stroll."

"Took you long enough," Tisdan said.

The monsignor opened the cab door, inviting him inside. "I thought you might have decided not to accept our invitation."

"I want this done," he said. "This has gone on long enough." He climbed into the cab. The monsignor followed him in and sat across from him.

"How is my daughter?"

"Safe."

The cab pulled through the gates of a walled courtyard, as the gates closed behind them. They drove on a winding path through dense woods. Trees, so rare to see in any part of the city, grew here with abandon. He fought the urge to gape at the forest around them.

They stopped at the coach house, with several other carriages. There was a place for each cab so that they all were parked undercover and protected from the elements. The coach house, hidden in the darkness outside, connected to the main house by way of a tunnel. A secluded fortress obscured from the furthest views.

The monsignor tapped Tisdan's shoulder with his cane. "This way, young man."

The tunnel was well lit. Sconces fueled by aether light lined the walls. The floor was marble, smooth, without a trace of dirt or dust. Tisdan had been singing an old nursery song in his head, something he heard a mother sing to soothe a child once. It stayed with him over the years, a song he thought a babe should hear. They arrived at a foyer before he had reached the second verse.

The walls were simple, plain, nothing of what Tisdan had expected. A butler dressed black coat and tails met them inside the foyer. He silently took the monsignor's hat, and helped him out of his travel cloak as well. He ignored Tisdan, a pointed slight that bristled at the base of his neck.

The next room assaulted the senses with its audacity. Elaborate scroll work along the baseboards and dark woods were offset with more aether light that hovered without a visible source; heavy fabric curtains had been drawn closed over the windows along a far wall; bookshelves lined another wall. The space appeared unnaturally clean, every surface scrubbed free of life. The grand entryway branched off to hallways that lead in opposite directions and a stairway that lead to an upper floor.

"We are expected in the east wing," the monsignor said. He followed the left hall out of the entryway. The walls were lined with paintings and tapestries. Items too large for a quick snatch and grab. They passed several doors as they walked the hall way, stopping at the door on the very end. He knocked three times, a pause between each knock.

The room had shelves of books along the walls, so many books that they were stacked on top of each other where they did not fit on the shelves. Papers and several open books were littered over a large oak desk in front of the book shelves. Wing back chairs with glass end tables faced the fireplace on the left wall. Smoke rose from one of the chairs near the fire.

They stood in front of the desk and waited. No words were exchanged, except for the occasional puff and then exhalation of smoke from the chair. Tisdan searched the room, his gaze moving from the papers on the desk to the various books opened in front of him and then to the book cases. He lost count after the first couple of shelves. After what felt like an eternity, the man stubbed out a fat cigar in the ashtray beside his chair.

Shadows clung to him as he stood, light filtered around him in a way that made him appear larger, imposing. The room itself was there to serve his needs. Tisdan and the Monsignor were simply a part of the room. The man's eyes and the features around them held Tisdan's attention. A youthfulness that didn't quite fit into this man's world stood out to him. He had expected older, grayer, power that could only come with age. Instead he faced a man in his early thirties who was still active and alive. The man circled around them without saying anything. He stopped in front of them on the other side of the desk.

"You have something that rightly belongs to me," he said. "How do we remedy this situation?"

"If it belonged to you, you'd already have it."

The man smiled, "I don't think you understand the situation properly." He came around the desk, now standing right next to Tisdan. "The amulet is mine. I have no time for the games of petty thieves."

Tisdan noticed something in his eyes. His life on the street had taught him the one thing that it seemed those who lived in high town had never learned. He had bluffed enough people in his life and been bluffed himself. Maybe it was a twitch, or a flicker in the eyes. But it was there for that moment, long enough to see it. This man hid behind the magic, the power he held in the crystals. But deep down he was nothing more than a child begging for a toy he thought his own.

"I came here today, prepared to do the honorable thing," he said. "I never meant to kill that man in the market. I never meant to hurt anyone. I do what I do to survive." A battle of wills, no magic, no one pulled from the aether for aid. Tisdan looked him straight in the eye and did not falter. "You have set your dogs to hunt me down. They return to you again and again without their prize. It is only when I voluntarily come to you that you are a breath away from what you seek. And still can't have it."

"Impertinent--" he began.

"You look for answers in things you do not understand. And have no clue when they are right in front of your face," Tisdan said. He pulled the amulet from his sash and placed it on the desk in front of the man. "Take it, it will never reveal itself to you. You will never be able to unlock the power it holds."

As the amulet left his hand, he stepped away from the desk. The temperature in the room dropped in a rush. The fireplace blew out with a cold wind. Fog blew in through the chimney filling the room. Tisdan stepped through the doorway into the aether, closing it as he passed through.

He closed his doorway behind him, cut them off from pursuit. They could not trace him, could not go where he had gone. His mind full of thoughts of Jillian and where she lay sleeping, guided him back to where he had started. He was in the world and stepping through the door into the building in the space of a heartbeat.

Jillian lay still asleep where they had made a makeshift bed, where he hoped she would be. He kneeled beside her, and gave her a quick shake. "I'm back," he said. "They have what they wanted. Little good it will do them."

She rubbed the sleep from her eyes, looking up at him. "But how," she asked.

"They have no idea what it is," he said. "They'll never figure it out."

She crossed her arms to ward off the cold, "How can you know that?"

He smiled and sat down beside her. "The amulet doesn't have any power," he said. "It isn't like the crystals the shapers use to harness the aether. The amulet is a key, a key to a specific lock." He opened his hand palm up. A small blue flame grew in the center of his palm. He set the flame on the ground beside them. It grew giving them warmth deep to their core without burning what it touched. "Ever notice the different shapes on the edge of a key? They become useless when you change the tiniest detail."

###

ABOUT THE AUTHOR

Jon M. Jefferson is a longtime fan of Science Fiction and Fantasy stories in all their forms. He has spent most of his life looking for magic in the everyday moments of life. He hails from the tundra of Southwest Michigan. The monsters in his life include his wife, two daughters and two granddaughters.

Printed in Great Britain
by Amazon